ZOAYLAND

The Adventure Begins

Maelyn Drew

ISBN 979-8-88751-109-2 (paperback)
ISBN 979-8-88751-110-8 (digital)

Christian Faith Publishing
832 Park Avenue
Meadville, PA 16335
www.christianfaithpublishing.com

Printed in the United States of America

Chapter 1

Once upon a time in a humble little house, there lived a young boy named Elzafan. A bit small for his age, he had golden-blond hair and bright blue eyes as clear as the summer sky. The fellow's smile was contagious.

Elzafan was the youngest of four children, having two older brothers and one sister. Since his older siblings had moved out on their own, only his mother and he lived in the little brick house they called home. His daddy left him when he was four years old and moved far away. Although Elzafan was a timid little lad who was quieter than most nine-year-olds his age, he loved talking to his best buddy, King.

King was a big brown German Shepherd with soft dark eyes, a black nose, and large pointed ears. He was a lovable dog and a great listener. Because of his great love for Elzafan, King was very protective of him. The two of them spent every free moment together. They had already been through a lot together, but that was nothing compared to the adventure ahead of them!

Gathering a few slices of sandwich bread from the wooden breadbox in the kitchen, Elzafan put them into a clear plastic bag. *Mama won't mind if I use just a little bit for bait*, he thought as he went out on the patio in the backyard. It was a bright and early Saturday morning, not too hot or too cool. The temperature was just right. Perfect, to be exact. Elzafan was doing what he loved to do every weekend.

Racing down the steps, King was quickly by his side. He rubbed King's head, saying to him, "Let's get ready to go, boy!" Walking to the gray outbuilding, they both went inside. Elzafan grabbed his silver fishing reel and small tackle box. After putting them and the bait into his blue backpack, he left the building and walked toward the gate. Unlatching it so King and he could leave, he closed it back once they were out.

Elzafan let out a loud shout so his mother could hear him through the screened living room window, "Mama! King and I are going down to Big Pond, okay?"

She shouted back to him, "Okay, be careful and make sure you are home in time for supper. I love you."

"Okay. Love ya too," he said as he headed down the dirt driveway.

Now, Big Pond was just a short trip from his house, less than a twenty-minute walk ahead. Down the hill they went across a couple of the neighbors' yards and a small creek. About halfway there now, just a gravel road and field with freshly plowed red dirt was left to cross.

Reaching the other side of the field, they took a trail that went into the woods. Carefully going down a steep bank, they made it to the bottom and followed the rocky creek that led to Elzafan's favorite spot. Though it was called Big Pond, the pool of water was not that deep.

When a big rainstorm would come, a lake that was far upstream overflowed and sent lots of water downstream. Not only would water fill the creek, but plenty of fish also came with it! Since Big Pond was the biggest pool of water in this creek, it held the most fish. Anyone who loved to fish would say it was a "honey hole." This meant you could always catch fish there. Elzafan mostly caught bluegill here, and the biting was always good. Sometimes, he would even get lucky and catch a bass!

There was one reason above all others why Big Pond was such a special place. His big brother Elijah showed him this spot and had taken him there many times when he was younger. It was at Big Pond where Elijah taught him how to fish with just a reel.

Finally reaching the tiny pond, Elzafan and King stood there in silence for a minute. The trickling sound of water flowing around rocks and into the pool was pleasant to hear. This quiet and peaceful moment was quickly interrupted when they heard a mighty wind rushing through the trees. It was coming right at them! King began to bark loudly as they tried to brace themselves. One gust of wind blew so strongly against him that it knocked him off-balance.

With nothing to hold on to, he yelled, "King!" and fell backward into the water.

Chapter 2

Crawling out of the hole into the bright sunshine, the little red ant shouted, "Another day my Maker has given, and I'm thankful for it!"

Born deep underground, Johnny grew up in this red ant colony on the hill. Unlike some of the others in his community, he believed and followed the instructions that his ancestors had passed down to them. Every ant in the colony could learn from these writings called the Golden Leaf Scrolls. However, only a few cherished them.

The elder red ants before them said the scrolls contained sacred teachings from their Creator. To study and follow these truths would make one wise.

To Johnny, this was a great treasure. He was sure the founders of their colony had guidance from one who was much greater than themselves. After all, they had settled and built the anthill on a great piece of land. It had endured through many generations, even when it seemed like it was going to be destroyed at times! This place called home that Johnny and the others enjoyed was from the wise ways of their ancestors, the elder red ants.

Hearing the splashing sounds of fish jumping out of the water, Johnny gazed down at the huge blue lake in the valley below. Surrounded by bright green meadows, this beautiful scene reminded him every day how blessed he was to live here. It was a magnificent place indeed. And it was called Zoayland—the land of life, a world of miracles! In this great land, animals, birds, and insects talk like people. Here, their language is love. Many creatures in Zoayland even sing and dance.

Yes, Zoayland is a glorious kingdom with a wonderful Prince to care for it. His name is Arneon, the Crimson Lamb. His father, Alpha, gave him Zoayland to reign over. The Crimson Lamb wanted all the creatures in His kingdom to love Him and each other, but everyone was given the choice. Would they choose right or wrong?

Many creatures in Zoayland chose to follow Arneon. However, some did not. Sadly, this caused trouble in this land of life, Johnny was different, however. He was a courageous, little red ant who was filled with faith, hope, and love. He believed that his ancestors got the Golden Leaf Scrolls from Father Alpha and His son Arneon. With all his heart, he wanted to honor Prince Arneon in the way he lived.

Leaving the anthill, Johnny headed down a well-worn path that went through a patch of green weeds. He had traveled this way many times before, but today was not like any other.

Suddenly, there was an unsettling sound in the distance. This made Johnny's red antennas stand up on his head. "Is that laughing that I hear?" he wondered.

The closer he got to the bottom of the hill, the louder it became. As he went around a large, jagged rock, Johnny was troubled by what he saw.

There was a scared little blue ant with oversized antennas. The poor creature was tied to a twig that was sticking out of the ground! He was surrounded by a bunch of other ants who were picking on him.

One of them yelled loudly, "Your antennas are bigger than the twig you are tied to!"

The others stood there laughing.

Another ant spoke up, saying, "We don't like blue ants with big antennas."

As they continue to bully and poke fun at the little blue fella, tears began to run down his face. The mean and hurtful things they said made him feel ashamed, alone, and afraid. All he could do was lower his head and stare at the ground.

As they were taunting him, Johnny came running and got in between them. "That's enough!" he shouted. "Just because he's not like you doesn't give you the right to pick on him."

"But he is funny looking and has weird antennas. He doesn't belong here," they protested.

Seeing the angry looks on their faces, he answered, "Even though he's a different color, he is still our neighbor."

Another red ant quickly asked, "Why are you taking up for this stranger?"

Johnny wisely replied, "My Creator teaches me to love Him with all I am and to love my neighbor as myself. This means doing unto others as I would want done to myself. How many of you want to be treated the same way you are treating this blue ant?"

Everyone became very quiet as those words sank in. Feeling sorry for their wrongdoing, one by one, the red ants turned and walked away.

Now Johnny and the blue ant were the only ones left standing there.

Chapter 3

Landing flat on his back, Elzafan made a huge splash and quickly sank to the bottom. Seeing his best friend under the water, King swiftly dove in after him. The boy opened his eyes and saw what looked like the surface of the pool. He quickly started swimming toward the light and noticed this passageway was very narrow. Feeling like he couldn't hold his breath much longer, he swam with all of his might! Glancing back, he saw his loyal dog paddling right behind him.

Elzafan knew Big Pond wasn't deep, and he wondered why it was taking so long to reach the surface. Just then, he realized it was an underwater tunnel they were swimming through! He could see a light up ahead, and it was getting closer. Pressing on, he thought, *Almost there!* Finally, he made it out of the water, gasping for fresh air!

King came up beside him, and he was breathing hard too. Climbing out of the pool together, they stood and rested on the rocky bank. Elzafan took off his backpack and set it on the ground. Still a little dazed from what happened, he looked at King and asked, "What was that all about?" His lovable German Shepherd responded by shaking the water out of his thick, hairy coat. He sprayed water everywhere!

"Easy, boy," Elzafan said with a giggle. Now his attention returned to his surroundings. He had always admired the scenery at Big Pond, but now everything looked different. It all appeared clearer! Colors were much brighter too! The water in the stream and pool sparkled radiantly. It was the most beautiful blue he had ever seen! The chirping sounds from the birds in the trees was clearer also. It was like new music to his ears.

Elzafan sat down on the ground and took the bread out of his backpack. Squeezing the plastic bag to make sure it was airtight, he was glad the bait was still dry. Soggy bread would fall off the hook every time! Opening another pocket on his backpack, he got out his trusty silver-and-red fishing reel. It was soaking wet, so he turned it upside down and drained the water out of it. After this, he opened the clear plastic bag, pinched off a piece of bread, and rolled it into a tight ball with his fingers.

Putting it on his hook, he glanced at King and said, "This stuff works every time." Elzafan pushed the cast button on his reel and swung the ball of bread over the pool. Releasing the button with his thumb, the bait made a *plop* sound when it hit the water. Letting it sink, he waited with great excitement. He would always put his index finger under the line so he could feel any vibration when a fish nibbled on the bait. In less than a minute, he felt a little tug on the line! Bracing himself to get ready, he said, "There he is." When the fish tugged a second time, he quickly pulled up on the reel. The fight was on! Slowly and steadily, he reeled in the line. This seemed like one of the hardest fighting fish he'd ever hooked at Big Pond. It almost pulled the reel out of his hand!

Suddenly, the fish came to the surface, thrashing and splashing water everywhere! Elzafan was able to pull the fish out of the water, and up to where he was standing. When he got a hold of it, he put his reel down with the other hand and gently took the hook out of its mouth.

"Ouch!" the fish said loudly.

"What?" Elzafan asked, taking a closer look at it. The fish was bright blue with orange stripes down its sides.

With the deep voice of a man, the fish replied, "Why do you look so puzzled, little man? Do you know there's a purpose? For you, there's a plan."

Astonished, the boy answered, "Uh…I've never heard a fish talk before. And I have never seen a tiger fish here either."

Standing up on its tail in the palm of Elzafan's hand, the tiger fish exclaimed, "Boys and girls did not come from some animal. You're no accident, as some people say. Adamkind is the Maker's creation. He's the Potter and they are the clay!"

Looking around with great wonder, the boy asked, "Where am I?"

Holding out his right fin for a handshake, the fish answered, "My name is Oscar, though it's a surprise. Welcome to Zoayland, a world of the wise."

Awkwardly shaking Oscar's fin with his pinky, he said, "My name is Elzafan."

Leaping out of his hand into the water, Oscar popped his head up and replied, "Be brave, little man. I'm glad to meet you. This fall you have taken will lead to what's true."

Chapter 4

Using his mandibles to cut the little blue ant free, Johnny said to him, "I'm sorry that my fellow ants have mistreated you." As he turned and started walking away, the blue ant hurried along to catch up with him.

Coming up beside Johnny, he asked, "Why do you treat me like an ant from your own colony?"

Johnny stopped and looked at him before answering, "Alpha made all ants equal. Red, yellow, black, and white. The blue ones and all the other colors to."

The blue ant was very surprised at what Johnny had said and asked, "But why are some ants mean to others who are different?"

Johnny wisely replied, "Because they choose to live their own way instead of Alpha's way."

Now the blue ant's antennas were standing straight up when he answered, "I have heard about this Alpha you speak of. If this Creator teaches you to love your neighbors, then he must be good."

Johnny quickly reassured him, "He is good, and His mercy endures forever."

The little blue fellow reached out one of his antennas to him and said, "My name is Azul, my friend."

Touching antennas, Johnny replied, "I'm Johnny."

As they walked down the path together, Azul thought that he could learn a lot from Johnny about this good Creator. Reaching the edge of the pond, they heard a strange sound nearby. Unsure of what it was, they walked faster in the direction it had come from. Now when they got closer, it became clear to them. It was the sound of a voice!

"Help! Someone help me!"

Looking at Azul with astonishment, Johnny replied, "Somebody's in trouble."

When he said this, both started running. They left a cloud of dust behind them!

"Right there, Johnny," Azul yelled, pointing his long antennas toward the water.

Both quickly stopped when they saw what was floating in the water. It was a big black widow spider on a bright green leaf!

The red and blue ants trembled when they saw her.

Uh-oh, Johnny thought to himself.

Now the spider was too far from the shore to reach dry land by herself. She needed help! Spiders were very dangerous to ants, so they always stayed away from them.

"We must be very careful," Azul warned.

Suddenly, they were frightened by a voice that growled, "I know y'all aren't gonna help her!"

Looking out over the water, they saw a dark-green snapping turtle on a log. Glaring at them with piercing red eyes, she said, "Think about all the wrong her kind has done to the ants."

Johnny responded by saying, "Spiders may be our enemies and many have wronged us, but we should not seek revenge."

With a noisy hiss, the turtle snapped and said, "What nonsense! An eye for an eye and a tooth for a tooth is what I say. I don't forgive or forget. I get even!"

Turning to Azul, Johnny replied, "Alpha forgives and forgets our wrongdoing when we confess it to Him. We should forgive others too, even our enemies." After saying this, he used his mandibles to cut down a huge green weed.

The two ants worked together, pulling it to the edge of the pond. Putting one end of it into the water, they pushed it out to where the spider was.

When it reached her, Johnny yelled, "Grab on to it!"

The spider latched on to it with her strong front legs. Johnny and Azul worked together as they slowly pulled her to the shore.

Reaching land, she crawled off the leaf and safely onto dry ground. Staring at the red and blue ants for a moment, she replied, "No one has ever been so kind to me. Thank you!" Quickly going on her way, she disappeared under some big rocks nearby.

This nice peaceful moment was suddenly interrupted when the snapping turtle yelled, "No mercy! No mercy! That's the way I live! And I do not! I will not forgive!"

Johnny had a look of sadness on his face when he spoke to Azul, "If we forgive, then we will be forgiven. But if we don't forgive others, Alpha will not forgive us. Those who are merciful will receive mercy."

"What is mercy?" Azul questioned.

Happy to know that his new friend wanted to learn, Johnny answered, "Mercy is not getting what we deserve."

Looking at the turtle, Azul asked, "Why are there only a few who forgive and show mercy?"

Johnny wisely replied, "Only a few realize they need Alpha's mercy and forgiveness just like everyone else."

Chapter 5

Izafan thought about what this spunky little tiger fish had said. He had been coming to Big Pond for as long as he could remember, but this was the first time he'd fallen in. That unexpected wind made him lose his balance! He had never felt the wind blow that hard at Big Pond. Something strange had happened, but he wasn't sure what had taken place. He wondered about what Oscar meant when the fish said, "This fall you have taken will lead to what's true."

Looking at Oscar, the boy asked, "Why am I here?"

With a bright twinkle in his eye and a warm smile, the tiger fish answered, "Let us go, little man. There is much you must see. This answer you shall find. Now come and follow me!"

As Oscar turned to head downstream, Elzafan quickly put his reel and bait into his backpack. Strapping it on, he followed his new friend who led the way. King was right behind him. The boy felt very peaceful and happy as he walked beside this beautiful freshwater creek. If girls and boys were made for a purpose just as Oscar said, then Elzafan wanted to know why he was on earth. Maybe here in Zoayland, he would find out what was true. Feeling a very strong sense of adventure, he was excited about this mission he was on.

Oscar stayed ahead of them, zigzagging from one side of the creek to the other. Occasionally, he would jump out of the water and back into it. It was like the tiger fish was in his very own playground! After going downstream for what seemed like half an hour, Elzafan saw a huge tree on a hill far away. It was glistening in the bright sunlight. He stared at it in wonder because this was the biggest tree he had ever seen!

As they came closer to it, Oscar leaped out of the water and landed on the boy's shoulder. Elzafan was astonished. He'd never seen a fish that could jump like this before! He listened carefully as Oscar spoke.

"Look, little man, at that giant tree. It's there you must go, for there you shall see."

"What should I do when I get there, Oscar?" he asked.

The tiger fish replied, "When you get to the tree, knock on its trunk—one, two, three." After saying this, Oscar jumped back into the bright blue water and quickly disappeared.

Chapter 6

As Johnny and Azul went down the path beside the pond, they heard singing in the air above them.

"I am a bumblebee. That's me. I am Bumby the bumblebee!"

Looking up, they saw a yellow-and-black bee flying as fast as a dragonfly! With an oversized body and tiny wings that buzzed loudly, he closed his eyes and swerved left and right.

Azul shouted to him, "Look out!"

But it was too late. *Crash!* The bumblebee ran straight into a patch of bright-colored flowers and tumbled to the ground. Johnny ran to him, hoping that he was okay.

As he was getting up off the ground, fluttering his wings, he exclaimed, "What a landing!" Looking at Johnny, he blinked his eyes and said, "My name is Bumby, and I've got news to tell. I heard a snake say that Oscar is a bad little tiger fish."

"I have met Oscar, and he's a good fish," Johnny quickly replied.

"Well, well, I've got news to tell! I heard—"

"Wait a minute," Johnny said before the bumblebee could finish. "It's wrong to spread rumors about others like you are doing."

"Isn't that what gossip is, my friend?" Azul asked Johnny.

"Yes, it is. It's never wise to do this. It causes others to think bad thoughts about someone that may not even be true.

Bumby spoke up and replied, "But when I spread pollen around, it helps flowers grow and be healthy."

Nodding his head, Johnny continued, "That's right, pollen is good for plants because it helps them. But gossip is bad, and it hurts others. It's like spreading poison around to every plant. Gossip is not good for one 'self or others. It's harmful to everyone involved."

After hearing this, Bumby took off in flight, singing, "I am a bumblebee. That's me. I am Bumby the bumblebee!"

Now gossip was a big problem among the blue ants. Every day, Azul heard ants talking bad about each other and spreading rumors. This bothered the little blue fellow, so he asked, "Why do we want to say bad things about others more than good things?"

Johnny looked at him and answered, "Our own pride. When we think of ourselves as better than our neighbors, then we feel like it's okay to belittle others. The only time we should look down on someone is when we are trying to pick them up."

Chapter 7

Gazing up the hill where the tree stood, Elzafan and King headed in that direction. The scenery around them was beautiful. *This is amazing*, Elzafan thought. The grass was deep dark green with shades of purple along the surface. He could feel a gentle breeze as red, yellow, and blue birds twirled and chirped around him. It all seemed like a dream.

When they reached the giant tree, they gazed up at it in wonder. It towered over them and looked like it grew into the clouds! Every limb was filled with golden acorns that sparkled in the bright sunshine. Elzafan and King stood there in awe for a moment. Remembering what Oscar had told him, he reached out and gently knocked *one, two, three*. Silence filled the air for a moment. Then suddenly, he heard a voice. "Whooo is it?"

Glancing at King in disbelief, he answered, "My name is Elzafan."

It was quiet for a while before the voice replied, "I know whooo you are."

At this saying, a hidden door on the tree began to open. Walking inside, the boy and his dog were astonished at what they saw!

Chapter 8

Starting on their way again, Johnny and Azul could see all kinds of fish swimming in the pond. There were green, yellow, and orange fish everywhere. As they swam in circles, it looked like they were performing a peaceful dance. Then, the ants heard something through the weeds next to them. It sounded like it was heading their way!

"What is it?" Azul asked.

Looking in the direction of the sound and then at each other, they said together, "A hoppy toad!"

Suddenly, a big green hoppy toad with bright-red eyes came crashing through the weeds. Johnny yelled, "RUN!"

Quickly, they headed toward a leaf that was floating on the edge of the water. The hoppy toad was gaining on them fast! Before jumping onto the leaf, Johnny grabbed a piece of straw that was on the ground. The two were moving so fast when they landed on the leaf, it caused them to surf out farther onto the water! Johnny used a piece of straw to paddle them across the water. The toad had just made it to the edge of the pond and jumped in. *Splash!*

"It's heading our way!" Azul cried out.

"When we reach those tall weeds, we've got to climb up as fast as we can," Johnny answered.

The toad was quickly catching up with them. It was drawing closer and closer! When they made it to the patch of weeds, Azul jumped off the leaf and crawled up the weed lightning fast. Johnny quickly climbed up backward, pulling the leaf out of the water with his mandibles. They both climbed high enough where the toad could not reach them.

"We made it, Johnny!" Azul shouted joyfully.

Now the hoppy toad was below them, swimming back and forth as he stared up at them. He stopped and floated for a moment. He was trying to think of a way to get them! As he was in thought, there was a sudden splash in the water where the toad was floating. Something grabbed his leg and tried to pull him under! This frightened him so much that he quickly swam away and was seen no more.

Azul asked, "What pulled the hoppy toad's leg?"

Taking a deep breath of relief, Johnny replied, "Hoppy toad wanted to eat us, but a fish wanted to eat him!"

Chapter 9

Standing before them was a big white owl. It shined like a pearl! With bright yellow eyes, it studied them carefully. The owl's head swayed from left to right before saying, "My name is Hoot and I know whooo you are, me lad. The important question is, do you know whooo you are?"

All the boy could say was, "Well...Elzafan."

With a jolly chuckle that made him bounce up and down, Hoot replied, "'Tis true! Your name means 'God of treasure.' Like all children, you are treasured, me lad."

A small tear trickled from the boy's eye when he heard this. "But if I'm treasured, why did Daddy leave? I don't understand why he wasn't there for me."

With kindness in his eyes, Hoot looked at him and said, "Humans have not always lived right, me lad. Even though your daddy made some wrong choices, it doesn't mean he did not love you. You are made in the image of Creator Alpha. You are loved and treasured!"

Wiping the tears from his eyes, Elzafan looked at King and asked, "Like I treasure him?"

Nodding his head, Hoot replied, "Far greater, me lad."

Now Elzafan remembered that Oscar had mentioned Adam to him. "Mr. Hoot, who is Adam?"

The wise white owl continued, "When the Creator breathed the breath of life into Adam's nostrils, he became a living soul. From this first man, the Creator made all people who live on earth."

Elzafan thought about this for a moment. It was Oscar the tiger fish who told him, "Boys and girls did not come from an animal. Not an accident as some people say. Adamkind is His crowning creation. He's the Potter, and they are the clay."

Now Elzafan had heard at school that people started out as animals and developed into humans over time. "But Mr. Hoot, where does it say that people are made in the image of a Creator?"

"Why, me lad, it is in the sacred book called the Holy Bible. Earth is filled with them!" Hoot exclaimed.

Elzafan had heard about the Bible, but he never saw one at home until his mother started going to church. He remembered learning some of the names of the books from the Bible, but he didn't know anything else. Nobody read it to him or shared it with him either.

Hoot continued, "The first book in the Bible is called Genesis. In chapter two, Alpha brought every creature to Adam for him to name them. What Adam called them, that was their name. Now, me lad, the reason you have entered Zoayland is to find and follow the truth. Beware, Elzafan, son of Adam. There are powers of darkness that will come against you. Be watchful and wise! You must journey all the way upstream. It will take some time, but eventually you will reach the great blue pond. At the top of the hill beside it, you will discover a large anthill. It is there you'll find a red ant named Johnny. Just tell him I sent you."

"Thanks, Mr. Hoot. I'll do that," Elzafan said as he headed out the door.

Before it closed behind them, Hoot shouted, "Remember, lad! You are loved and treasured!"

Chapter 10

Climbing back down the tall weed, Johnny placed the leaf back onto the water. "Azul, before you come down, will you cut off a piece of the weed from the top? I need it to paddle us back to shore."

The little blue ant climbed to the top, clipped it with his mandibles, and brought it back down to Johnny.

"Thank you, Azul," Johnny said as he began to paddle them back to the bank.

The two ants really enjoyed this peaceful ride back. There was no hoppy toad in sight! Reaching land, they jumped off the floating leaf and walked together along the path. It wasn't long before the quiet was interrupted by the sound of a high-pitched voice.

"Johnny! The one who is made in the image of the Creator has come. He's here in Zoayland!"

The ants were surprised when they saw a beautiful pink butterfly land beside them. Her yellow spotted wings fluttered as she gazed at them with sparkling green eyes.

"How do you know this, Noofie?" Johnny asked her.

Blinking her eyes quickly, she replied, "I was downstream resting in a tree near the little blue pool. Suddenly…I heard a splash! Then I saw him and his furry friend come out of the water!"

Now Johnny had a puzzled look on his little red face, so Azul asked, "What's wrong, my friend?"

"I was just thinking about this one that Noofie has seen. I have read about the sons of Adam and how many of them turned away from their Maker."

"But look at me, Johnny. I'm an example that our Creator can transform any creature. Who would have thought that I'd be the butterfly that I am today? When I was a caterpillar, all I did was crawl around and chew up everything in sight!" Leaping into the air and flying in circles, she sang, "In the Lamb, I am. In the Lamb, I am. In the Lamb, I am a new creation!"

Johnny and Azul giggled together as they watched Noofie twirl in the air. When she landed back on the ground, Johnny introduced them. "Noofie, this is my new friend, Azul. Azul, my good friend, Noofie."

"Nice to meet you," the little blue ant replied.

She quickly answered, "It's a pleasure to meet you too."

Johnny continued, "You are right, Noofie. Our great Creator can change anyone. His works are wonderful!"

"Yes indeed. I'm excited about this great news. A son of Adam has come to Zoayland! Well, my friends, I must get home. Hope to see you again soon!"

"See you later, Noofie," Johnny shouted as she lifted off.

Azul smiled and waved goodbye with one of his antennae.

Looking at Azul, Johnny said, "If you have time, I would like to invite you to my home."

"I would be happy to join you, my friend," the little blue fellow answered with a bright grin.

As the two of them walked down the narrow path that went through some tall green weeds, Azul thought about what he had learned. It was good to treat others the way you want to be treated. And showing mercy to others, even one's enemies, was the right thing to do. He wondered what he would learn next. He knew for sure that Johnny truly loved his Creator and others. It showed in how he lived his life, especially when he stood up to those bullies and helped him. Johnny had been like a big brother to him. When others chose to be mean, Johnny chose to be good to him. *Oh, that everyone would be kind to each other*, he thought as they headed to Johnny's house.

Chapter 11

Elzafan and King turned and headed back down the hill toward the stream. The trickling sound of the water became louder and clearer as they got closer to it. Everything around them was so peaceful and relaxing. Huge rocks were all along the sides of the creek. There were red, white, and blue ones everywhere! Elzafan was startled when he heard a loud splash. As he looked around him, King had disappeared. His German Shepherd had jumped into the water! He smiled as he watched his dog lap up water with his tongue. *There are many beautiful creeks and lakes back home too*, he thought to himself.

King climbed out of the stream, and as usual, he shook the water out of his thick hair. Elzafan looked up into the bright blue sky and saw a flock of white and gray doves flying over them. Some were landing in the trees nearby. As they continued walking along the side of the creek, Elzafan could see lots of red, blue, and yellow fish swimming in the water.

It reminded him of Oscar, the talking tiger fish. He hoped that they would meet again. It all still seemed like a dream to him. Up ahead, he could see they were getting close to the place where they began. It looked almost like Big Pond! As they passed by the pool of water, he said to King, "So that is the doorway in and out of Zoayland!"

They had gone a long way upstream when King started growling very loudly. The hair on the back of his dog's neck was standing up as he stared at something in front of them. Looking in that direction, Elzafan was surprised when he saw a big black snake hanging from a tree. It gazed at them with glowing red eyes that never blinked.

Flicking its silver tongue out a few times, the snake calmly said, "I've never ssseen you before. Who are you?"

"My name is Elzafan."

"Elsssafan. Hmm…my name is Mr. Sssight. Do you know where you are?"

"I have been told this place is Zoayland," the boy answered.

As his head slowly moved from side to side, the snake asked, "Who sssaid thisss?"

With a look of doubt on his face, Elzafan replied, "The tiger fish did."

With a sly grin, Mr. Sight rolled his eyes and continued, "Ahh…and I'm sure his name is Ossscar. The little fish who talksss about a Creator who has a purpossse for girlsss and boysss. It makesss me sssick to my ssstomach. I don't believe in it if I cannot sssee it! Have you ever sssseen thisss Creator that Ossscar ssspeaks of?" Now the snake had a big smile on his face when he asked this question.

Before Elzafan could answer, a strong gust of wind was felt all around them. Looking up, they saw a huge black-and-white eagle swooping down. It landed between the snake and Elzafan. It was bigger than him!

Glaring at the snake with golden colored eyes, he asked, "Do you believe that you have brains, Mr. Sight?"

"Sssure, I do," the snake replied.

The eagle boldly exclaimed, "So you do believe in things you can't see!"

At that, the snake slithered down the tree and into a patch of tall weeds nearby.

Turning to the boy, the eagle introduced himself, "My name is Abraham, but you can call me Abe."

"Nice to meet you, Abe. My name is Elzafan, and this is my friend King." Looking at Abe with amazement, he continued, "You are the symbol of America, my country. Our sixteenth president had the same name as you!"

With a strong deep voice, Abe proclaimed:

Abraham Lincoln was an honest man.
He trusted that Almighty God,
His Maker had a plan.

Abraham Lincoln was a man of care.
He called upon Americans,
To join him in prayer.

Abraham Lincoln was someone who stood tall.
He knew united people stand,
Divided they will fall.

Chapter 12

Johnny and Azul were now climbing the hill that led to the little ant's home. As they headed along, Johnny said to Azul, "My ancestors believed in their Creator and built our home on this great piece of land."

"That is good to know. Some of the blue ants that founded our colony believed in their Maker too," Azul replied.

When they finally reached the top, Johnny said, "Welcome to my home."

After saying this, he and Azul crawled into the hole. Going down one of the tunnels, they entered Johnny's living room. There were small pools of blue water throughout the room with red ants relaxing around them. Some were even swimming and playing in the water! Azul was astonished at how peaceful it was here. He followed Johnny to a table that was filled with pieces of fruit.

As they sat down, Johnny said, "Help yourself, my friend."

The little blue fellow picked up a small piece of banana with his mandibles and took a big bite. "Yummy!" Azul mumbled with a mouthful of the sweet fruit.

Johnny began to chew on a piece of cherry as they watched some other ants playing in the pool. Looking at Azul, he said, "In a little while I would like to show you something."

"Okay, Johnny." Now Azul wondered just what it was that Johnny wanted to show him. It was very kind of him to invite Azul into his home and share a delicious meal with him. He had never been treated this well by ants from a different colony. Azul could tell that Johnny was one of the leaders here too. All the other red ants deeply respected him.

After they finished eating, Johnny asked, "Are you ready to see something very special?"

"Yes, my friend!" Azul answered with a big smile.

They left the table and went into another tunnel. Deeper and deeper, they went into the ground. Johnny and Azul crawled down this tunnel for a while until they reached a large open area. The little blue ant was amazed at what he saw! The whole room was filled with a golden glow. There was a big acorn in the middle of this room. It looked like it was made of solid gold! Slowly walking up to it, Johnny carefully opened the door on the front of it. He reached inside with his mandibles and pulled out a beautiful golden scroll. Placing it on a table nearby, Johnny unrolled it and put a stone on each end to hold it open.

As both of them gazed at it in silence, Johnny said, "This is one of our sacred Golden Leaf Scrolls. Our ancestors passed them down to us."

With a look of wonder, Azul asked, "Where did they get them from?"

"They received the scrolls from Alpha, our Creator. His son Arneon gave them to my people long ago." After closing the scroll and putting it back into the acorn, Johnny asked, "Do you have any other questions, Azul?"

"Well...I do have one more, Johnny. Who is Arneon?"

The little red ant smiled at him. "I thought you would ask about him. Arneon is the Prince of Zoayland. He's a red Lamb that has three white horns on His head. His eyes are bright gold; and each one of his hooves are a different color: red, yellow, black, and white. Because He is the color of reddish purple, Arneon is often called the Crimson Lamb."

For a moment, Azul stood there in silence as he thought about what Johnny said. He wanted to know more but decided to ask later. The little blue fellow couldn't stop thinking about this Lamb he'd heard about. In his heart, he wanted to see Arneon with his very own eyes. Maybe he would get to see him—just maybe!

Chapter 13

Gazing at the big German Shepherd, Abe asked, "Where did King get his name from?"

Elzafan's face lit up when he answered, "We named him that because he protects our yard. Not only that, but he also pulled a dog off me one time when I was being attacked. When I yelled his name, he came running to rescue me!"

"I see he's been a loyal friend to you," Abe replied.

"Yes, and the best friend a boy could ever have."

After hearing Elzafan's answer, the big eagle continued. "Trust in the Creator with all of your heart, son of Adam. The serpent knows that your mind is a wonderful gift from your Maker. Be watchful, for you will be tempted to fear and doubt. Always remember to walk by faith and not by sight."

Elzafan suddenly remembered hearing this before and asked, "Why do people refuse to believe, Abe?"

With a look of concern upon his face, Abe explained. "Some people have faith in their own knowledge and ways more than anything else. You see, a proud heart can cause someone to think highly of themselves. So highly, they begin to believe that they are more clever than our Creator. It's a very serious condition to be in, but it is a choice they have made."

Stretching out his massive wing and pointing upstream, he continued, "You see, believers are like a fish that swims upstream. Any fish can simply float downstream. But it takes faith and firmness to overcome the currents of fear and doubt. That's what fighting the good fight of faith is about."

"I've heard that saying somewhere in my world," Elzafan said as he thought about it for a moment. "'Fight the good fight of faith' is found in the book called Timothy, chapter six. It is in the New Testament of the Bible. You see, most fighting is never a good thing, but the fight of faith is a good fight!" Abe exclaimed.

Now Elzafan knew how to read and write, but he had never read the New Testament. "I have a lot to learn," the boy replied as he looked at Abe.

The big eagle smiled and continued, I believe that is why you are here in Zoayland, son of Adam. This wonderful land of life is filled with truths that you will learn. There are many friends that you will meet also. Just remember, there are other creatures that will try to lead you astray."

Looking around him, Elzafan was surprised to hear this. It was hard for him to imagine any wrongdoing in such a beautiful place. Remembering what the white owl had told him, he replied, "Abe, Mr. Hoot said I needed to find a little red ant named Johnny."

"Good idea! Mr. Hoot is a great friend of mine, and he's a wise, 'ole bird too!" Abe chuckled and then continued, "A friend will always try to lead you in the right way. If someone is trying to lead you in the wrong way, they are not being a true friend to you."

"I never thought of it like that," the boy answered.

Stretching out his huge wing and pointing upstream, Abe said, "About a mile that way, you will find Johnny's home. Continue your journey, Elzafan, son of Adam. Be strong and courageous."

As the giant eagle leaped from the ground and flapped his powerful wings, his voice deeply roared, "Praise the God of Abraham!"

In time, Abe was completely out of sight. "Let's go, King," Elzafan said as he started walking on his journey for the truth.

As they went along, he thought about his dear mother, Lindsdon. He wondered if she had been looking for him. After all, it seemed like he had been here in Zoayland for a while now. A couple of years earlier, he got lost at the beach for hours, and his mother cried until he was found. He didn't want to worry her by being gone too long. Although he never wanted to worry her again, Elzafan just had to continue his quest for the truth.

Finally, they reached the big blue pond. It was beautiful! He had seen many ponds back home, but none of them could compare to this one. It was filled with bright blue water, and you could see almost all the way to the bottom of it.

As they enjoyed this moment together, Elzafan yelled, "Look King!" Coming their way was a bright pink butterfly. As it got closer, the boy held out his hand. He was astonished when it gently landed on his hand. He giggled and said, "Hi there. Do you talk too?"

Surprisingly, the butterfly leaped in the air, twirled, and sang, "In the Lamb, I am. In the Lamb, I am. In the Lamb I am a new creation!" Landing on his hand again, the butterfly replied, "Hi, my name is Noofie."

Gazing into her sparkling green eyes, he answered, "Nice to meet you. My name's Elzafan, and this is my buddy King. I am looking for the home of a little red ant named Johnny."

Blinking her eyes and fluttering her wings, she replied, "Oh, my friend Johnny lives right up the hill from here. I would be happy to show you the way."

"That would be great. Thanks!" he answered.

Taking off from his hand, Noofie exclaimed, "Follow me!"

Chapter 14

Johnny and Azul made their way back up the tunnels and came out of the anthill. As they stood on the hump of red dirt together, Johnny said to Azul, "Look."

The little blue ant squinted his eyes and saw a pink object in the distance. "What is it?" Azul asked, waving his oversized antennae in the air.

"Why, Azul…I think it's a friend of mine. It looks like Noofie! Is that someone following her?"

As they got closer, Johnny could see the boy's golden-blond hair shining in the sunlight. "Created in the image of Alpha. He is a son of Adam," he said to himself. The little red ant's heart began to race! This was the first time he had ever seen a son of Adam in Zoayland, so this was a very special moment.

When Noofie reached them, she yelled with excitement. "Johnny! Look who I have found." Landing in front of them, she fluttered her wings and smiled.

Johnny looked up and saw the boy's face. His eyes were bright blue! Squatting down, the boy replied, "Hey there. My name is Elzafan. Mr. Hoot sent me here. Are you Johnny?"

"Yes, I am Johnny. It's a pleasure to meet you, Elzafan. This is my home, and these are my friends, Noofie and Azul."

Elzafan continued, "It's great to meet you all. Mr. Hoot said that I would find the truth here and learn wonderful things that I don't know."

"Everyone who seeks for the truth will find it. Please wait here for a moment," Johnny said before he crawled into the ant hole.

As everyone waited for him to return, they heard something hitting the ground. It was a thumping noise. One thump, two thumps, then a few more.

Elzafan was surprised when he saw red apples, oranges, purple grapes, and lots of other fruit lying on the ground. There was also fresh bread all around. All of this was falling from the sky!

Everyone looked up and saw black ravens flying above them. After the birds had dropped the last bit of food from above, they flew away. They were all astonished at what had just happened.

What's going on? Elzafan thought to himself.

Just then, Johnny returned with the Golden Leaf Scroll and carefully laid it down. When the little red ant saw the food on the ground, he asked, "Where did all this come from?"

Still having a shocked expression on his face, Elzafan replied, "When you left, a flock of ravens flew over and dropped it all around us. It was like they did this on purpose."

Johnny's eyes widened as he looked at Elzafan. "Our Maker is great, and He is good. I believe He has provided this food."

The boy picked up some bread and answered, "From His hands we are fed. Let us thank Him for this bread. Mama and Daddy used to say that before we would eat. I was only about two or three back then, but that memory is still there."

Now when King saw Elzafan enjoying the food, he grabbed a big piece of bread with his mouth and started gobbling it up! Everyone laughed when they saw the bread dangling out of King's mouth. As soon as the big German Shepherd finished off the bread, he quickly got another one.

Elzafan looked at Johnny and asked, "So where do we start?"

Carefully unrolling the scroll, Johnny replied, "Let's begin with the question, where did I come from?"

Chapter 15

The tiger fish swam quickly upstream, zigzagging around rocks and jumping over other ones that were in the way. Pushing himself along with his strong tail, the oncoming blue and white water was no match for him. Oscar was born to swim!

Even though he was one of the toughest fish who lived in this stream, he wasn't the biggest one. There was one fish that Oscar had to be aware of. It was the silver-skinned catfish, also known as "catdaddy." They were the biggest and baddest fish in this place. They usually stayed deep underwater because they did most of their eating on the bottom.

There was one good thing that Oscar knew about these big old catdaddies, they were not as fast as he was. Even then, the spunky little tiger fish still had to watch out for them. He never wanted to be caught by surprise. Oscar continued heading upstream toward the pool where he met Elzafan. He wondered about how the boy and his dog entered Zoayland.

Finally, he reached the blue pool of water. Up ahead, he saw a tunnel that went into the rocky bank. Oscar had heard from many others how there was only one way the sons and daughters of Adam could enter the kingdom of Zoayland. Looking at the tunnel, Oscar thought, *Narrow is the gate, Our Prince did say. Into His Kingdom, There's only one way*.

Carefully and slowly, he swam into this passageway. As he got closer to the end, he began to swim faster. Reaching the surface, Oscar flipped his tail back and forth quickly and jumped out of the water. Instead of landing on his tail and standing up as usual, he flopped onto his side. *Gasp!* He couldn't breathe!

Frantically, he flopped a few more times, trying to stand up on his tail again. Oscar needed air, so he kept flipping and flopping on the rock. He was getting closer and closer to the edge of the pool! Desperately, he thrashed some more until finally, *ka-blop!* He was back in the water and able to breathe again.

The little tiger fish was shocked at what had happened. He didn't know why he wasn't able to breathe. Oscar was sure that he had entered Elzafan's world at the other end of this tunnel, but he'd never experienced anything like this before. He was so happy it was over and he could breathe again. Dashing back through the tunnel in a flash, Oscar was glad to be in Zoayland once again.

Chapter 16

Now deep within the realm of Zoayland, there was a forbidden place called the forest of gloom. A handsome gray goat flew down from the sky and landed upon a tall green hill. Folding back his big white wings, he stared at the snakes that were gathered around him. His piercing black eyes had bright silver slits in the middle of them. On his head were two large golden horns that slightly pointed back. Stomping his front hoof down in anger, he exclaimed, "I am Malvor, ruler of this forest! I will be obeyed and followed. Just like the Prince of Zoayland!"

"But what about thossse who choossse to follow the Lamb massster?" one of the snakes asked.

Snorting loudly, he yelled, "Hush! I cannot stand such thoughts! These creatures follow this Prince by faith and love. I will not put up with this!"

Together, the snakes asked, "Massster…what do you have in mind?"

Lifting his head up proudly, he grinned and laughed with a deep voice. "Ahh my little serpents. I've got just the plan."

* * * * *

"Here it is," the little red ant said as he looked closely at the scroll. Everyone quietly gathered around so they could hear what Johnny had to say. "In the beginning, Elohim created the heaven and the earth."

"Hey! That word has the same first two letters as my name," the boy replied.

Studying the scroll for a moment, Johnny looked up and answered, "Elohim means the Supreme God. Your name comes from this word, and it means God of treasure."

"I remember Mr. Hoot told me that I was loved and treasured, but I have made many mistakes. How can this be?" Elzafan asked as he stared at the ground.

"His love for you is far greater than any mistakes you have made. The Golden Leaf Scroll also says that God made man in His image and likeness. You are a descendant of Adam, the first man," Johnny explained.

"So that's why everyone has been calling me a son of Adam!" Elzafan's eyes widened when he said this.

Johnny nodded his head and continued, "Yes, the Creator has made all nations of people that are on the earth from this one man."

The boy quickly asked the little ant, "Where did girls come from?"

Searching the scroll for a moment, Johnny answered, "God caused Adam to fall into a deep sleep, removed one of his ribs, and made a woman from it. She was Adam's wife and her name was Eve. They lived together in a garden called Eden and had lots of fruit trees to eat from. There was only one tree they were not supposed to eat from. It was called the tree of the knowledge of good and evil. Their Creator warned Adam that if he ate this fruit, he would surely die."

With a scared look on his face, the boy asked, "Didn't Adam stay away from this tree?"

Studying the words in front of him, Johnny replied, "The Golden Leaf Scroll tells the story..."

Chapter 17

Oscar knew where to find Abe, the mighty bald eagle. Far downstream, the river ran into the great lake. Very often, Abe would fly over this huge body of water. There were times when he could be seen above the place, soaring gracefully. If it could be said that Oscar was made to swim, it could surely be said that Abe was made to fly!

Now there was also another creature who lived in the forest around this lake. Her name is Grace, the lovely gray squirrel. Grace was like a caring mother to a lot of the creatures in Zoayland, but to Abe, she was just like a sister. Whenever she needed to travel a far distance, all she had to do was blow her acorn whistle. Abe could hear the high-pitched sound from a very long distance. Even better, with his excellent eyesight, he could see for miles! With Grace riding on the back of the mighty eagle, she could travel as fast as the wind!

Oscar continued to swim down the river, passing many schools of blue, green, red, and yellow fishes along the way. The stream was filled with all sorts of different things. There were grayish-colored crayfish on the bottom with bright purple frogs swimming across the top of the water. As he got closer to the great lake, Oscar became more alert and careful. Entering this body of water was like going into a different world. Not only was it bigger, but it was also a busy place.

The little tiger fish leaped out of the water and landed on a rock at the lake's edge. Looking out across the water, he saw something that was flying toward him. Oscar was about to dive into the water by instinct, but he waited just a moment. As it got closer into view, he could see that it was his good old friend, Abe. The big eagle landed beside him with a powerful gust of air coming from his wings.

"It's good to see you, Oscar."

With a concerned look on his face, the tiger fish replied, "Through the tunnel is where I went. When I came out, my air was spent!"

"I understand my friend. The tunnel leads to Elzafan's world. It is different there. Here in Zoayland, you can breathe out of the water. In the boy's world, fish breathe underwater through their gills."

"I flipped and flopped, just to breathe air. Oh, my dear friend…it was quite a scare!"

Abe nodded his head. "I know this surprised you, Oscar. The only way you can breathe in the boy's world is by staying underwater. If you do that, you'll be able to breathe. Oscar, please stay close to Elzafan. He has gone upstream to meet with Johnny. You and I know how that old goat will try to stop the boy. We must look out for Elzafan and help in his quest for the truth."

* * * * *

While everyone focused on Johnny, the little red ant began to read, "Now the serpent was slyer than any beast of the field which the Creator had made. The serpent said to the woman, "Has God said, you shall not eat of every tree of the garden?" And the woman said unto the serpent, "We may eat of the fruit of the trees of the garden: But of the fruit of the tree, which is in the midst of the garden, God has said, you shall not eat of it, neither shall you touch it or else you will die." And the serpent said to the woman, "You shall not surely die."

"Johnny! The Creator told Adam he would die if he ate from this tree," Azul replied as his big antennae stood straight up.

Johnny was very proud of his new friend's answer. "You are right, Azul. The serpent lied to the woman."

Blinking her big green eyes, Noofie asked, "Why would the serpent do such a thing?"

Knowing that everyone around him wanted to hear the answer, Johnny explained, "The serpent is serving the prince of darkness here. This prince is an enemy of the Creator and His creation. His main purpose is to drive the sons and daughters of Adam away from God, their Father."

With a sad expression on her face, Noofie asked, "Why does he want to do this to God's family?"

"God the Creator is love, and He wants a relationship with all the sons and daughters of Adam. The prince of darkness knows this, but he does not have this love inside. That's why he seeks to keep people from God."

Everyone was quiet, so Johnny continued, "That day in the Garden of Eden, Adam ate the fruit that his Creator told him not to eat. This brought terrible things into your world, Elzafan. Before this, Adam and his wife only knew good. Now they knew good and bad."

Remembering a saying he had heard, the boy replied, "The first man's wrong came on all the human race. Our Creator had a plan, to save us by His grace."

Johnny was surprised that Elzafan had spoken this wise truth, so he responded, "That's correct! The wrong that Adam did is called sin. It was an offense because he didn't obey his Creator's command. This is why there is death in your world, Elzafan. But you have entered Zoayland to learn the way to eternal life."

After saying this, Johnny carefully rolled up the Golden Leaf Scroll and took it back into the anthill.

Chapter 18

Oscar knew his trusted friend Abe was right. Elzafan would need their help.

Abe said to him, "Well my friend, I'm going to find Grace and let her know about the boy."

Oscar responded by waving goodbye with his fin before diving back into the bright blue water.

Leaping from the rock, the huge eagle flapped his mighty wings. In an instant, he was far above the water and making his way across the lake. As Abe flew higher, he opened his wings and stretched them out. Soaring with the current of the wind, he began going in circles. Each time he went around, Abe lifted higher and higher. He scanned far below with his keen eyesight. Far off, he spotted Grace in the top of a very tall acorn tree. This was the acorn forest, a beautiful and peaceful place. When Abe saw her, he dove lightning fast and landed right above her.

Looking up, she asked, "Abe is that you up there?"

"Yes, Ms. Grace. It is I," he politely answered.

In a flash, she scurried up to where he was perched and replied, "Thank you for visiting me. Is everything well?"

"Well, Ms. Grace. I've got good news and bad news. The good news is a son of Adam has entered Zoayland. He is special, just as all girls and boys are. The bad news is the snakes know he is here. It won't be long before the goat finds out about this."

Grace sat up and replied, "*We* must not worry. The goat is mean and strong, but our Prince is loving and much stronger than him. Has the boy met with Mr. Hoot?"

"He has spoken with the wise owl. Mr. Hoot sent him to Johnny," Abe answered.

Looking at each other, they said together, "He will need our help."

* * * * *

When the little red ant returned, Elzafan asked, "How will I learn the way of eternal life?"

Johnny looked at the boy and replied, "The way cannot simply be discovered by oneself. It is only revealed to the hearts that sincerely seek it. You must journey to the acorn forest around the great lake. It is by Grace you will find the way, the truth, and eternal life. If Noofie is willing, we could lead you there."

"Yes!" she exclaimed as her wings fluttered.

Focusing on his little blue friend, Johnny continued, "Would you like to go with us, Azul?"

"Uh…my friend. I'm afraid to fly," he replied with a low voice.

"It's okay, my friend. Noofie is a careful and great flyer," Johnny reassured him.

"Okay Johnny. I'll go with you," Azul replied.

The butterfly was bigger than Johnny and Azul, so they climbed onto her back together. They looked like two ants on a bicycle!

With her high-pitched voice, Noofie yelled, "Hold on, my friends. Off we go!"

Landing on the boy's shoulder for a moment, Johnny said to him, "Follow us." After saying this, they took off once again.

"Let's go, boy," Elzafan said to King as they followed closely behind Noofie.

Her bright colored wings flashed as she flew. The lush green meadows around them changed from light to darker shades as the gentle breeze blew across the field.

Elzafan thought about some of the beautiful sights he had seen back home. Everything looked perfect in this place called Zoayland. It was wonderful! His thoughts were interrupted when Johnny called out to him, "Listen, Elzafan!"

Caw...caw...caw, came the sounds from the sky above them. Azul cried out in fear, "Oh no! It's the crows!"

Elzafan looked up and saw four huge crows with orange beaks. They were flying right toward them! "Run!" the boy yelled as he took off and headed for a patch of thick trees nearby. King was right on his heels.

"They're closing in on us!" Noofie shouted as she went even faster.

They were close to safety when everyone heard another loud cawing sound right over their heads. Suddenly...one of the crows swooped over the boy's head and went for Noofie. Quickly moving to the side, the crow's bite narrowly missed her! "Hold on tight!" she yelled to Johnny and Azul as they hung on to her back.

Now one of the crows had gotten a little too close to Elzafan, so King jumped high in the air and snapped at the bird. When King plucked out some of his feathers, he let out a loud squawk. King landed on the ground, spit out the feathers and barked loudly.

The crow squawked a few more times as it took off in the other direction. The other three took this as a warning and followed it.

"Good boy," Elzafan said as he rubbed King behind his ears. His dog loved it when he lightly scratched these spots!

Noofie landed on the boy's shoulder, and Azul said, "I'd say your furry friend ran that crow off for good, my friend."

"Yeah, King's my buddy, and he has always been protective of me," Elzafan replied.

"We have a little further to go before we reach the great lake," Johnny said to everyone.

Chapter 19

Oscar, the spunky little tiger fish swam throughout the lake toward the stream. Everything was going great until he saw a silver flash out of the corner of his eye. Quickly turning to see what it was, he was very surprised. A huge silver catfish was coming right at him with its mouth opened wide!

Thrusting as fast as he could with his tail, the little tiger fish dodged the attack. Now the chase was on! Zigzagging back and forth, Oscar easily stayed ahead of the catfish. Swimming around rocks and tree limbs that were along the edge of the lake, he was getting close to where the stream led into it. At this point, the current was coming against him very hard. He had to swim with all of his might! The closer he got, the slower he was able to swim. The catfish was right behind him! *Chomp…chomp!* The fish was biting at his tail.

Oscar knew he had a few more feet before he reached the mouth of the stream. He could see the water pushing through the two big rocks that were beside each other up ahead. He was almost there! Making one more push with all his strength, Oscar pressed between the rocks and into the pool of water behind them. The catfish was too big to fit through it, so he stopped. The spunky little tiger fish was safe! As he rested there for a moment, he knew his Creator had kept him safe once again. For that, he was truly thankful.

* * * * *

Taking off again with Johnny and Azul on her back, Noofie continued to lead the way. Elzafan and King followed closely behind. The boy felt a rush of excitement as he thought about learning the way of eternal life. He was starting to believe what his new friends were sharing with him. Being surrounded by so many loving creatures who cared about him, these new friends felt like family. Maybe there was a purpose for coming to Zoayland. Seeing a large body of water up ahead, he thought, *That must be the lake.*

When they finally reached the edge of the great lake, Noofie landed on Elzafan's shoulder. Johnny and Azul climbed off Noofie's back, looking at the beautiful scene around them. Everyone stood there for a moment, enjoying what they saw.

When a nice gentle breeze blew around them, Noofie replied, "The wind is a natural example of our Creator's Spirit. We cannot see it. But the effects of the wind can be seen when it blows upon the grass, trees, and water. Even though the wind and Spirit are unseen, they are just as real as things that we can see."

Everyone was quiet as they thought about what Noofie said.

"I remember something like that in the Golden Leaf Scroll," Johnny replied. "It speaks about the wind blowing where it will. Although we can hear its sound, we don't know where it comes from or where it is going. It's the same with everyone who is born of the Spirit." After the little red ant said this, he turned to Elzafan and continued, "Across the stream and around the lake, you will find the acorn forest."

Looking in that direction, the boy saw a path that he could follow. "Thank you all very much," he said to Johnny, Azul, and Noofie.

"We are happy to be able to help," the little red ant answered.

With a quick flutter of her wings, Noofie replied, "Be careful!"

Azul simply smiled and nodded his head to him. The red and blue ants climbed back onto Noofie's back, and off they went!

Looking at King, he said, "Let's go boy."

When they turned and headed down the trail together, Elzafan saw a big tree up ahead that was laying across the creek. It was a perfect little bridge for them. They carefully crossed over it and walked along the path at the edge of the lake. Finally, they reached the acorn forest. It was filled with tall oak trees that were towering above them. The happy sounds of birds chirping and singing could be heard all around. Elzafan wondered what he would learn in such a beautiful place. He remembered Johnny's words, "By Grace you will find the way, the truth, and eternal life." But he didn't know what that was. Hopefully he would find out soon.

Chapter 20

"Now listen to me. This is what I want you to do. You must find where Johnny keeps that Golden Leaf Scroll. Find this scroll and bring it to me!" Malvor snorted as he stared at the snakes around him.

One of them asked, "But Massster…how can we find out where the ssscroll is hidden?"

They all looked at Malvor and waited for his answer.

Shaking his head in frustration, he asked, "Do I have to tell you how to do everything? Find someone who knows where the scroll is first. Once they start talking to you about it, trick them into telling you where Johnny keeps it."

Now the gray goat had a sly little grin on his face.

The snake named Mr. Sight spoke up and asked, "What about the boy?"

"What boy?" Malvor asked as he focused on Mr. Sight.

"I met a boy here in Zoayland."

Now the goat was furious. "And you waited until now to tell me this? How foolish!" Malvor was breathing hard as he glared at the snake.

Mr. Sight answered in a soft voice, "Uh…he wasss by the ssstream. I tempted the boy to focusss only on what he could sssee until…"

"Until what?" Malvor asked.

"The big eagle ssswooped down and took up for the boy."

"Abraham!" Malvor yelled as he snorted and stomped his foot. "That fowl of faith has been like a thorn in my hoof for as long as I've known him!" It was quiet for a moment before Malvor continued, "Just bring me the scroll. I'll deal with the boy myself!" After saying this, Malvor spread his huge wings and quickly lifted off into the sky. Higher and higher he went until he was completely out of sight.

* * * * *

"Great is our Father God. Of your works we sing. Almighty is our Father God. The Lord is our King." Elzafan's mother loved to sing, especially when she was fixing supper. Even though most people knew her as Lindsdon, she was simply "Mama" to Elzafan.

Sliding a pan of buttermilk biscuits into the oven, she set the timer. After pouring a cup of coffee, she stirred some cream and sugar into it and sat down at the kitchen table. She thought about her dear children: David, Elijah, Angelica, and Elzafan. Three sons and one daughter. Lindsdon loved them all very much and did the best that she could with raising them. She even worked longer hours at a local restaurant just to pay the bills and put food on the table.

Every time she worked over, her daughter, Angelica, would take care of Elzafan. Although they were brother and sister, Angelica was just like a mother to him. Sometimes Elzafan would slip and call her Mama. Angelica would laugh when he did this. Even though they went through hard times, they loved one another and made it through together. Now that Lindsdon's two sons and daughter had their own homes, only Elzafan and herself lived here now. Finishing her coffee, Lindsdon got up and continued to prepare the evening meal. She wanted to make sure that supper was ready when her boy got home.

* * * * *

As Elzafan and King walked deeper into the acorn forest, they heard beautiful singing in a nearby tree. "To this world, the Father sent His Son for you and me. Upon a cross, He gave His life so that all could be free. These glad tidings we proclaim and lift our voice to sing. Glory to our God most high, for Christ our risen King."

Now their eyes were fixed on a wonderful sounding gray squirrel that was on a tree limb high above them. Quickly scurrying down the oak tree, she stood in front of them and spoke, "I have been expecting you, dear child. My name is Grace."

Elzafan smiled and replied, "Johnny said I would find the way by grace, but I didn't know what he was saying."

"Yes, Johnny is a very good friend and one of the wisest ants in Zoayland. He sent you to me so that I could show you the way of Zoay, that is, the way of eternal life." Pointing down a narrow path that went through the acorn forest, she continued, "Beyond this forest and through a valley, you will come to a mountain. It is at the top of this mountain through faith that you will receive eternal life."

With a puzzled look on his face, the boy replied, "But there's so much that I don't understand."

Her brown eyes were full of compassion as she answered, "Only believe, dear child. You will understand later."

Elzafan nodded to her and then asked, "How long has Zoayland been around?"

Grace smiled at him. "This kingdom has existed before the earth was made. Our Creator has no beginning and no ending."

"Wow!" Elzafan exclaimed. "It's hard to imagine that."

"That's because we are limited. Now, dear child, it is time to be on your way. I look forward to seeing you again." After saying this, she scurried up the huge oak tree and was seen no more.

Chapter 21

"Happy, so happy, I am to be. That ol' mean catfish didn't catch me!" Oscar said to himself as he swam in the fresh blue water stream. Now this spunky little tiger fish could follow it wherever it branched off. In many places, this stream would feed into larger bodies of water and continue to flow through them.

Swimming at a slow pace, Oscar thought about his new friend, Elzafan. He knew that boy had a purpose here even though he wasn't sure what it was. It was the first time he had ever met a son of Adam in Zoayland. Oscar was still a little troubled about what happened when he entered Elzafan's world. Remembering how he couldn't breathe caused him to tremble. It was comforting to know that he could breathe if he stayed underwater. For now, he would just stay in the stream and be patient. One thing he knew for sure, there was only one way in and out of Zoayland. He would wait for the boy to return to the pool. He hoped it would be sooner than later.

* * * * *

As his little blue friend climbed off Noofie's back, Johnny said to him, "We'll see you later, Azul."

"Adios my friends. Thank you for the ride home," he replied. Azul smiled and waved goodbye with one of his antennas as they lifted off and began to fly away. He was very happy that he had met Johnny and Noofie. They already seemed like family to him. "Thank You, my Creator, for these new friends," he said as Noofie and Johnny disappeared into the distance.

* * * * *

Mr. Sly, the yellow snake, curled up and waited quietly beside a patch of wildflowers. He was one of Malvor's best servants because he was tricky. Mr. Sly could pretend very well, and he could change colors whenever he wanted to. He knew this would be a good spot to find out where the scroll was. His bright silver tongue flickered out and back into his mouth as he lay in the sunshine. Suddenly, he heard just what he'd been waiting for.

"I am a bumblebee, that's me. I am Bumby, the bumblebee!"

The snake watched closely as the bee crashed right into the patch of flowers. After tumbling down a little bit, it climbed back up onto one of the flowers.

Buzzing its wings, the bee exclaimed, "What a landing!" Seeing the snake nearby, the bumblebee said, "My name is Bumby, and I've got news to tell. I heard someone say that all creatures in Zoayland are bad."

"I sssee," Mr. Sly replied with a grin on his face. "I have heard about a little red ant named Johnny. Have you ever ssseen him?"

"Why yes! I just talked to him," Bumby replied.

"I sssure would like to meet a good friend like Johnny. Do you know where I could find him?" Mr. Sly asked.

Now Bumby was happy to answer. "Well, I heard that he lives on the hill above the big blue pond."

"Outsssstanding. Thank you for the information." As Mr. Sly slithered away, he thought, *Thank you for ssspilling the beansss, Bumby*.

* * * * *

Elzafan and King started down the path that went through the acorn forest. This place was so wonderful and peaceful. The boy felt like he could stay here forever. His mind went back to home. He had been in some great places and saw some awesome things, but he loved the little neighborhood where he lived. Elzafan thought about his mother. "Was she worried about him? How long had he been away?" It seemed like he had completely lost track of time here in Zoayland. It was like time no longer existed.

Making their way through the forest, they came out into an open field. The view was magnificent! The bright green rolling hills stretched as far as their eyes could see. On the other side of the valley below them was a large mountain. This was exactly what Grace had said. Looking at his dog, he said, "There it is, boy."

King licked his hand and then focused on the scene in front of them. Elzafan slowly began to go down the hill with King following him. The closer they got to the bottom, the bigger that mountain appeared. Gazing up at it, Elzafan saw huge rocks that were flat and jagged. Others were round and smooth.

When they reached the valley, he felt a comforting gentle breeze. He smiled and took a deep breath of fresh air. They were now halfway across the valley. Green grass was all around them. Once they made it to the other side, the two of them started climbing the mountain together. Following the narrow path that led them higher and higher, Elzafan began to breathe harder. It was like some unseen power was drawing him upward on this journey.

Even though he couldn't explain it, the boy felt it deep within his heart. Someway, somehow, Elzafan knew that this was exactly where he was supposed to be. It was his destiny. All doubt and uncertainty melted away as he climbed. The words of Grace came to his mind, "Only believe, dear child. You will understand later." Finally, they reached the top. Elzafan and King were astonished at what they saw!

Chapter 22

Oscar had now made his way back upstream to the small pool of blue water. Looking at the underwater tunnel for a moment, he chose to be brave and swim into it. When he reached the other side, he took a deep breath and jumped out of the water, landing on a rock at the edge of the water. Oscar looked around. Elzafan's world was a lot like Zoayland, it seemed, but he knew that he couldn't stay out of the water too long. Feeling the need for fresh air, he quickly dove back into the pool.

Now Oscar was as bold as a lion, yet he also knew his limits. Living without oxygen was one of them! Suddenly, he had an idea. When he was standing on the rock, he could clearly see a stream of water flowing into the pool. Could he breathe in Elzafan's world if he stayed underwater as Abe said?

Oscar believed his trusted friend and what he told him. Taking a huge breath, he jumped out of the water and stood again on the rock. With all his might, he leaped from the rock and dove into the stream. Slowly opening his mouth, Oscar took in the water and let it flow through his gills. His bright blue eyes widened with surprise. He could breathe! Oscar carefully explored this new stream, but he made sure he didn't go too far in this unknown place. After just a few minutes of swimming around, he returned to the pool and went back through the underwater tunnel. Now he knew that he could enter Elzafan's world, and everything would be okay.

* * * * *

The happy pink-and-yellow butterfly landed, and Johnny climbed off her back. "Thanks for your help Noofie," he said to her with a smile.

"You're very welcome Johnny. I'll see you later," she replied. Blinking her lovely green eyes, she fluttered her wings and took off.

The little red fellow was so thankful to have such wonderful friends here in Zoayland. He thought of his new friend, the blue ant named Azul. Johnny looked forward to seeing him again and wondered when that would be.

Then he remembered Elzafan. There was something special about this son of Adam. Johnny felt like he'd known the boy all his life, even though they had just met. With all his heart, he believed the boy would need his help. Although he didn't know how, Johnny was determined to be there for him. The little red ant would stay closer to him than a brother.

Crawling down the anthill tunnel, he let the colony know that he would be gone for a while and said goodbye to everyone. When he climbed back out of the anthill, Johnny headed toward the creek. The fastest way to get downstream was to take his tiny green leaf boat. If he rode the swift moving water, he could reach the blue pool in hardly any time. Once he arrived, he'd wait for Elzafan to return.

* * * * *

Everything was silent as they gazed at what stood in front of them. It was a tree in the shape of a cross! Unlike all the other trees, this one was filled with colorful stripes: red, yellow, black, and white. The cross-shaped tree looked like a candy cane! Elzafan could see that it was growing out of a mound of solid rock. The very atmosphere on the top of this mountain was filled with a loving and peaceful presence. It was as if time had completely stood still for a moment.

Feeling goosebumps rising on his arms, Elzafan's heart started beating faster. As he gazed upon the cross-shaped tree, it was astonishing to see something standing behind it. It was slowly moving toward him! The closer it got, the clearer it became. What or who was this? Was this the one that would show him the way to eternal life?

* * * * *

The sly snake waited in the weeds, watching Johnny as he left the anthill. As soon as he was out of sight, crafty old Mr. Sly headed toward the anthill. Knowing he couldn't find and take the Golden Leaf Scroll by himself, he decided to get someone to help. All he needed to do was find a fallen tree nearby. There happened to be one close to Johnny's home.

The snake quickly moved toward it and stopped when he got there. With his forked tongue flickering in and out of his mouth, Mr. Sly found exactly what he was looking for. Termites! The tree log was filled with them! One of them was bigger than all the others. It also had huge teeth! Mr. Sly said in a gentle voice, "Excussse me, sssir. I have heard that you are sssome of the bessst diggersss around. Isss that true?"

"Well, uh...there ain't no mite that can dig better than me," the biggest one answered.

"Oh really? Do you sssee that anthill over there?"

Looking in that direction, he replied, "Yeah."

Mr. Sly continued, "There'sss a golden leaf ssscroll inside that anthill. I don't think you can dig down to find it."

The termite turned red in the face and answered, "Why…I bet ya I can!"

"I'll believe you when you bring me the ssscroll," Mr. Sly replied.

At that saying, the termite stormed off saying, "I'll show ya!"

* * * * *

Suddenly, King lay down on the ground. The big German Shepherd was acting like he was a puppy again! He rolled over and over as he wagged his long tail. Finally, Elzafan saw who it was that stood at this cross-shaped tree.

Right in front of him was a purplish, red colored Lamb. Each one of its hooves were a different color as well. One was red, one yellow, one was black, and the other was white. This Lamb had three horns on its head. They looked like bright shafts of light! The Lamb's eyes appeared to be pure gold. Elzafan was speechless as he gazed at this astonishing creature.

It said to him in a deep voice, "Behold the Lamb."

Suddenly, the boy was in what seemed like a dream. He was standing on a hill and looking up at a man who was hanging on a cross. He heard a voice say, "The Father sent His Son to be the Savior of the world."

Elzafan wondered why this man was on the cross. As he thought about it, a song could be heard all around him:

> I love you—Oh, I love you. I gave My life
> On the cross to set you free.
> I love you—Oh, I love you. Come home—
> Oh, child—come home to Me.

Without any doubt, Elzafan knew that this was God's call. Falling to his knees, he said, "Lord, I believe in you." Suddenly, it felt like someone poured warm oil upon his head. As love, joy, and peace filled his heart, all he could say was "Thank You, Jesus."

The scene changed, and Elzafan was now standing in a garden. He could see people carrying the body of Jesus into a tomb. A big stone was rolled over the entrance. Suddenly…the ground began to shake. It was a great earthquake!

Elzafan looked up and saw a mighty angel coming down from above. This angel rolled the stone away from the door of the tomb. When he looked inside, the tomb was empty!

The scene changed again, and now Elzafan was on a high mountain. Standing in front of him in a white shining robe was Jesus, the Son of God. There were prints in His hands and feet where the nails had pierced Him.

With love in His eyes, Jesus said, "I am He who lives and was dead, and behold, I Am alive for evermore. Amen."

Immediately, Elzafan was awakened, and he could see Arneon the Crimson Lamb again. As tears of joy filled his bright-blue eyes, the boy said, "Jesus saved me."

Arneon smiled, nodded his head and replied, "Son of Adam, it is for this purpose that you have entered Zoayland. Alpha has chosen you to share the good news that Jesus is the Savior of the world. Through Him, every daughter and son of Adam are welcomed into the Father's family. Now return to your world, Elzafan, and be a witness unto Jesus. He is the way of Zoay. He is the only way to eternal life."

Chapter 23

Quickly and quietly, the big and strong termite began to dig a tunnel into the backside of the anthill. Mr. Sly gleefully watched him from afar off. In hardly any time at all, he surfaced and headed back toward the crafty old snake. Dropping the Golden Leaf Scroll on the ground in front of Mr. Sly, he proudly said, "Just like makin' sawdust out of wood."

The tricky old snake looked at him and answered, "Well, I guesss you ssshowed me."

The termite turned to leave, saying, "I'm the best there ever was!"

As he walked away with his head held high, Mr. Sly thought, *Ah…but not the sssmartest for sure.* Taking the Golden Leaf Scroll with his mouth, the sly yellow snake slithered into the weeds and vanished out of sight.

* * * * *

"Woo-hoo!" Johnny shouted as he rode the fast-moving water downstream. His tiny leaf boat was like a kayak as he shot in between rocks and along the streams of water. The little red ant smiled and giggled when he felt the rush of wind blowing past him. Johnny was quickly approaching the pool of blue water.

Going over one final small waterfall, he landed safely in the peaceful little pond. Paddling his boat to the edge of the water, he crawled onto the bank. After pulling his boat out of the water, Johnny looked out over the beautiful blue pool. *So this is the portal that connects Zoayland to Elzafan's world,* he thought.

He had heard about the sons and daughters of Adam, but he never dreamed that he would meet one of them. Johnny's little heart was filled with excitement when he thought about Elzafan. He was surprised when something jumped out of the water and landed beside him. It was his good friend, Oscar!

"Hey there Oscar."

"I came here to wait for Elzafan. When he returns to his world, I believe that I should go with him," Johnny replied.

Oscar understood what he was saying and wisely responded, "Most certainly, Johnny. What you say is true. This boy we've met needs a good friend like you."

* * * * *

When Arneon disappeared right before his eyes, Elzafan thought about what just happened. As he gazed upon the colorful cross-shaped tree, understanding started to fill his heart and mind. Now he remembered what Johnny had read to him from the Golden Leaf Scroll. Adam was the first man that God had made, and they were together.

When Adam ate from the tree that God told him not to eat from, it caused them to become separated. It was by Jesus giving His life on the cross that God made a way for every son and daughter of Adam to be able to come back to Him. Now, everyone could become children of God through believing in Jesus, His Son! For God so loved the world that he gave his only begotten Son that whosoever believes in him should not perish but have everlasting life.

Looking at King, Elzafan said, "Now I know that God is my Father, and He loves me."

His big German Shepherd wagged his tail and licked the boy's hand.

Turning to leave, Elzafan replied, "Let's go home, boy."

* * * * *

"Outstanding!" Malvor shouted with glee as Mr. Sly placed the Golden Leaf Scroll on the ground in front of him. "Now that I have Johnny's sacred scroll, we'll see how that little red ant likes this!" the mean old goat declared.

One of the other snakes asked, "Why isss thisss ssscroll ssso important to you, Massster?"

Malvor glared at the snake and yelled, "I'm the only one who asks the questions around here! This scroll is nonsense, and that is that!" Picking up the Golden Leaf Scroll with his mouth, Malvor quickly lifted off and flew out of sight.

* * * * *

As Elzafan and King reached the bottom of the mountain, they began to make their way through the valley below. Seemingly out of nowhere, the sky began to get darker, and thunder could be heard. This was the first time Elzafan had experienced a storm here in Zoayland.

Looking off in the distance, he saw thick clouds gathering with flashes of white lightning among them. The wind began to blow harder, and the temperature became cooler.

King started growling as he stared at something far off in the distance.

"What is it, boy?" Elzafan asked, looking in that direction. The hair on the back of his dog's neck rose. Now the boy knew something was wrong. As he continued to focus on the scene in front of him, Elzafan could hardly believe what he saw coming their way!

Descending from the sky was a beautiful gray goat. It had huge powerful wings like a Pegasus! Gracefully landing in front of them, they were silent and amazed at this wonderful-looking creature.

With piercing black-and-silver eyes, he gazed at Elzafan and said, "I am a mighty prince and have come to show you great things. I will answer your deepest questions. I will cause you to become a powerful one."

Elzafan asked, "But how can you do these things?"

With a look of confidence he replied, "It cannot simply be told, but I can show you. Will you come with me, dear boy?"

Glancing at King for a moment, he said, "It will only be for a little while, boy." His dog responded with a whine. "It's okay, boy. I'll be back soon," Elzafan replied.

The gray goat softly said, "Now climb on my back, dear boy, and you will fly like an eagle."

When he got on his back, the goat stretched out its big white wings. With just a few powerful strokes, they were high in the air, disappearing into the clouds above.

* * * * *

Saying goodbye to Johnny, Oscar jumped back into the water and headed downstream. The little red ant would do the best that he could to be a real friend to Elzafan. After all, true friends help each other and are there for one another. Friends try to keep each other out of trouble. Johnny knew if someone was trying to get him to do wrong, they were not being a true friend. He had met some who only pretended to be his friend, and it would be that way for Elzafan too.

In Zoayland, Arneon the Crimson Lamb taught them to love their Creator with all of their heart, mind, and strength. Also, to love their neighbors as themselves. But Malvor was a creature that was full of selfish pride and rebellion. He rejected the truth and love of Father Alpha and Arneon His son. Malvor refused to follow the good and right way and chose to do wrong instead. Johnny remembered reading in the Golden Leaf Scroll: "Do not follow the path of wrongdoing, and don't go in the way of mischief."

The little red ant was very thankful for the wise instructions he had been given. He knew that he had avoided lots of trouble by obeying the truths in the Golden Leaf Scroll. Now he wanted others to live in the good and right way too.

Chapter 24

King whined as he stood in the valley alone. He longed to be with his best buddy Elzafan. Not knowing where this flying creature had taken the boy, being separated from him was almost too much to bear.

The big German Shepherd was getting more and more restless. Then, he heard a comforting voice behind him say, "King."

Turning around, he saw Arneon the Crimson Lamb standing there. Walking up to him, the Lamb put his forehead to King's. When their heads touched, King heard these words on the inside, "You are Elzafan's loyal friend. Use this gift to help him." King's eyes got bigger as he realized what was happening. He started growing very fast! Within seconds, he had grown to the size of a huge bear!

Now King was looking down at Arneon who said to him, "Watch over and protect the boy."

King nodded to him and turned to go. The giant dog took off as fast as a racehorse!

Arneon smiled as he watched King quickly clear the valley and disappear into the forest on the other side.

* * * * *

The gray goat landed upon a high mountain and let Elzafan off of his back. The boy stood and looked around in wonder for a moment. Even though it was such a beautiful place, Elzafan did not have peace in his heart about being here. On the inside, he felt like he had made the wrong choice for coming here.

The majestic gray goat asked him, "What brings you here to Zoayland, dear boy?"

"I was fishing down at Big Pond just like any other day when I fell into the water. When I came up, I was here in this place."

"Mm-hmm...and I'm sure you have been told that you are loved and are here for a purpose, too." Malvor tried his best to hide the look of disgust on his face when he said this.

Elzafan continued, "Well, yeah. I met the Crimson Lamb at the cross-shaped tree. When I saw Him, it was shown to me that Jesus loves all the children of Adam. He died on the cross for our wrongdoing so that we could be forgiven."

Malvor huffed and said, "But you've got to remember all of the wrong you have done."

At that moment, Elzafan began to see some of the scenes of his past. It was just like watching a movie. There was a picture of him getting into a fight at school. Another one showed him taking candy from a store and not paying for it. He saw another one where he told his mother a lie.

Scene after scene replayed the wrong things he had done. Feeling shame and regret about these things, he bowed his head and stared at the ground. What could he say? After all, he had not always been a good little boy, even though he wanted to be.

The goat continued, "See, you must remember all of the naughty things you have done."

Before Elzafan could say a word, he heard a deep growl behind him. It rumbled like thunder! Looking up, the boy saw a terrified look on the goat's face.

Slowly backing away, Malvor softly said, "Easy boy. Easy now." After backing up, Malvor quickly took off in flight and got out of there.

Elzafan was startled at what had just happened. He was really surprised when he turned around and saw what was behind him!

* * * * *

Lindsdon finished preparing supper and gazed out of the kitchen window. *Maybe he's on his way home*, she thought. Walking out on the front porch, she yelled, "Elzafan, come home!"

Often, when he was late for supper, she'd call for him like this. With her high-pitched voice, he could hear her from afar off!

His mother knew if he was nearby, he'd hear her and come home soon.

* * * * *

Johnny had waited beside the small pool of water for a while now. He wondered how much longer it would be before the boy arrived. Surely, Elzafan would want to return to his world. Could it be that something had happened?

The little red ant knew all too well that ol' Malvor and his followers would do whatever they could do to stop the boy. Thankfully, there were many good creatures in Zoayland who would lend a helping hand to Elzafan.

As Johnny thought about neighbors and friends helping each other, he remembered his new friend Azul. It was such a great blessing to meet the little blue fellow. Perhaps he could go and visit him when he returned to Zoayland. Johnny wasn't sure if this was a good idea though. After all, he was different, and the blue ants might not accept a red ant like him.

Although he really wanted to see Azul again, it would be wise to trust in his Creator and wait on Him. In His time, the two of them would meet again.

* * * * *

Elzafan could hardly believe his own eyes! Was he dreaming? There in front of him stood a giant German Shepherd. It was his best buddy, King! "Whoa!" the boy exclaimed.

King lay down in front of him and looked into his eyes. Elzafan wrapped his arms around King's thick neck and hugged him. "Thanks for helping me, boy. How did you become so big?" Elzafan was amazed at how huge his dog was.

King responded by licking him on the side of his face.

Elzafan giggled, "Okay, boy, okay." At that moment, he had an idea. Climbing onto King's back, he said to him, "Get up, boy!"

The dog stood up with such ease. It was like the boy wasn't even on his back. "Whoa! You are strong as an ox, King." Elzafan balanced himself as his dog started walking around. It also seemed like King's senses were sharper. He knew how to carry Elzafan on his back like a horse does its rider.

After walking around a little bit, Elzafan said to King, "Go fast!"

At his command, King took off running. They quickly reached such a high speed that everything flew past them in a blur! Elzafan was astonished and filled with wonder. His best friend now had extraordinary abilities.

When Elzafan said, "Slow down," King instantly responded and settled into a steady gallop. Patting him on the side of his thick neck, he let King know that he appreciated him. "Let's go home, boy."

Instinctively, his dog turned and headed in a different direction.

Chapter 25

"That Crimson Lamb has done it again! Always getting in my way," Malvor huffed, stomping his hoof on the ground. All the snakes around him were as quiet as mice. With a mean grin, the goat snarled, "Ahh…but I still have Johnny's Golden Leaf Scroll."

One of the snakes asked, "What shall we do, Massster?"

"You ask some of the silliest questions!" Malvor shouted. "Go tempt others to hate their Creator and each other. Stop them from loving Him and one another! Whatever you must do, we have to turn all creatures away from following the Lamb."

* * * * *

"My friends. I tell you the truth. This red ant was different. He did not judge me because I do not look the same as him," Azul reassured all the blue ants that were around him.

One of them asked, "But why do we hate and fight with others that are different colors?"

"My friend Johnny said it's because we choose our way instead of our Creator's way," Azul replied.

Another little blue ant asked, "What is the Creator's way?"

Azul remembered what Johnny had said and he answered, "To love our Creator with all of our hearts and to love our neighbors as we love ourselves."

Another ant questioned him, "And who is our neighbor?"

Azul told them the story. "There was a little blue ant that was on his way home one day. Sadly, he was caught by some other ants and tied to a twig. They picked on him and said mean things that made him cry. As he cried out for help, there came a red ant out of nowhere! He bravely stood up to those bullies and cut the blue ant free. Which one was a neighbor to the little blue ant?"

It was very quiet for a moment before one of them answered, "The red ant who showed him mercy."

Nodding his head to them, Azul replied, "We should go and do the same."

Chapter 26

King and Elzafan reached the small blue pool of water in what seemed like no time at all. Lying down on the ground, his dog let him off his back. Elzafan was amazed when King returned to his normal size right before his eyes.

Looking at the German Shepherd, he asked, "How did you do that?"

King gazed at the mysterious pool and then back at him.

Elzafan looked at it too and began thinking about how it all began right here. As he stood there, Johnny quietly crawled onto his shoe and climbed up his pant leg. When he reached Elzafan's backpack, he managed to get inside unnoticed. He would have to hold his breath until they made it to the other side. Elzafan began to slowly wade into the water. "Here goes," he said before taking a deep breath and going underwater.

Opening his eyes, there it was! The portal. As he started swimming through it, he thought about how this secret tunnel had been there all along. If he had not fallen into this pool, the wonderful world of Zoayland would not have been discovered. Glancing back as he swam, there was King dog-paddling right behind him. No matter where he went, his loyal shepherd was always close by him.

When they reached the other side and came out of the water, Elzafan wiped his eyes to clear them. Climbing out and onto the bank, they stood there for a moment. As he looked around, Elzafan quickly recognized the tall green pine trees and the scenery. This was the world he had been born into, and he was happy to be back. Although everything was beautiful here, it couldn't compare to the wonderful world of Zoayland. His thoughts were interrupted when King shook the water from his fur, spraying it everywhere!

Elzafan giggled, saying, "Okay, boy! Okay! Let's head home."

They walked up the trail that went alongside the rocky creek. It twisted and turned through the woods until they reached a steep hill. Climbing up, they made their way out of the forest and down the old gravel road. Crossing a freshly plowed field of red dirt, Elzafan saw his neighbor's big apple tree up ahead.

Every summer, it would produce red apples that were juicy and delicious! When they became ripe, the apples would fall from the tree limbs and cover the ground. There was something even more interesting about this apple tree in Ms. Votterbell's backyard. It was the meeting spot where Elzafan and a very good friend enjoyed each other's company. Getting closer to the house, Elzafan hoped that his mother wasn't worried. After all, he had been gone for what seemed like days. He felt like he'd completely lost track of time. How would he explain what happened?

* * * * *

Her reddish-brown hair shone as the yellow rays from the sun beamed down on her head. Jezia was a bright and bold little eight-year-old girl. She was one year younger than Elzafan, and they were good friends. A tomboy at heart, she loved a lot of the same things that he liked: climbing trees, catching crawdads from the creek nearby, and running throughout the neighborhood.

Plucking a ripe purple muscadine from the vine in her yard, Jezia squeezed the fruit open and ate it. They were so delicious. It was hard to eat just one! She was an only child with a loving mother who took care of their home and a dad who was a full-time truck driver. Her parents had bought this two-story house that sat on a big plot of land.

From the looks of the place, the people who lived there before were probably farmers. There were four old outbuildings, lots of peach trees, and a spot where a garden use to be. Jezia and her friends loved to eat those fresh peaches from the trees every summer. Even though Elzafan loved his home, he really liked playing at Jezia's house even more. There was so much more space to run, play, and have fun. Jezia and Elzafan were as close as two peas in a pod. The truth be told, they were childhood sweethearts!

* * * * *

When they got home, Elzafan patted King on the head and told him to sit. The German Shepherd quickly obeyed, always willing to impress the boy. "Give me howdy."

At this saying, King lifted his front leg, putting his paw in Elzafan's hand.

"Good boy!" Opening the gate, he let King into the backyard. He closed it behind him and walked up the patio steps that led to the back sliding door. As soon as he opened it, the delicious smell of freshly baked homemade biscuits filled the air. Sliding the door shut, he said, "Mama, I'm home." He waited for her to answer.

"I'm in the kitchen, Elzy Poo. You are just in time for supper."

Now the nickname Elzy Poo was his mother's way of calling him her baby boy. When she called him by this name, he knew Mama was happy and everything was okay. Even still, he was a little surprised at her answer. If he was home by suppertime, this meant that he had been gone for only a few hours! He couldn't understand how this was possible. It felt like he'd been in Zoayland for days. At least one whole day for sure. Maybe time passed by much faster in Zoayland.

Whatever it was, he was glad to be home on time. Before going to talk to his mother, Elzafan went to his room and put on some dry clothes. When he came into the kitchen, his mother smiled and said to him, "You know you're my baby, don't ya?"

He grinned and nodded to her. This was his silent way of letting her know that he understood. Although he had gone through some rough times when his daddy left, his mother's love was one good thing that had never failed.

"Be sure to wash up before supper," she reminded him.

"Okay, Mama."

Going to the bathroom, he washed and dried his hands before coming back and sitting down at the kitchen table.

Lindsdon brought their plates of food and sat across from him. Reaching out and taking his hands in hers, she prayed, "Our Father in heaven, You are great, and You are good. We thank You Lord for our food. Amen."

His mother had prayed before their meals all the time, but something seemed different to Elzafan. He now had a deep sense of being thankful in his heart. There were many things he was thankful for: his mother and the rest of his family, clothes and shoes to wear, a good place to live, and a bed to sleep in. There were more blessings than he could count!

Looking down at this delicious meal in front of him, he thought, *God has been good to us*. He had a thick slice of roast beef with buttered mashed potatoes, corn on the cob and seasoned green beans. And finally, he had a big golden-brown homemade biscuit that was made just for him. His mother would make one that was twice as big as the others. Elzafan was the one who gave her the idea one day as he watched her press them onto the pan. From then on, Lindsdon would add one jumbo biscuit to every batch she made.

After finishing supper, they enjoyed a piece of pistachio cake with green icing for dessert. Elzafan and his mother worked together, clearing the table and carrying the dirty dishes to the kitchen sink.

As his mother began to wash them, she asked, "Does King have fresh food and water?"

"I'll go make sure, Mama," he replied before heading out the back door. As soon as he made it outside, his good friend was there to meet him. "Let's go get you some food and water, boy."

King followed him down the steps and into the yard. Pouring out the old water from the green five-gallon bucket, Elzafan refilled it with fresh cold water with the garden hose. Before the water reached the top of the bucket, King had his head in it and was lapping it up as fast as he could!

After Elzafan filled King's bowl with dog food, he put the bag away and went back into the house. Now it was time for him to have a nice warm bubble bath!

After finishing up, he got dressed and went to his room. He lay down on the bed and stared at the ceiling for a moment. It all still seemed like a dream. It also felt like one of the longest days he'd ever had. His thoughts went back to Zoayland and all the new friends he had met in that wonderful place. Feeling his eyes getting heavy, he closed them to rest. In hardly any time, Elzafan dozed off and was fast asleep.

Chapter 27

Johnny quietly crawled out of Elzafan's blue backpack and looked around. Seeing Elzafan lying there asleep, he thought, *This must be his home*. When he climbed down the backpack, the ground underneath him felt unusual. It was a soft and thick dark blue material. He had never seen anything like this before. Making his way up a big brown structure, he was astonished when he saw an exact copy of Elzafan's image. There was also a woman standing beside the boy. She had her arm around him and was smiling brightly.

Johnny wondered at this for a moment before noticing some other items: a white ball with red stitching that sat inside a large black pouch. There was also a small box made from wood. Peering across the room, he saw a round white-and-black object hanging near the boy's feet. It looked like some type of protection for one's head. Above Elzafan was some type of device with six blades, quickly and quietly turning. Johnny could feel a light breeze coming from it. To the little red ant, this was a strange place indeed! He would stay here throughout the night and return to Elzafan's bag in the morning.

* * * * *

"Wake up, Elzy Poo. It's almost time for school."

Slowly opening his eyes and squinting, he yawned and answered, "Okay, Mama."

Getting out of bed, he went to the bathroom to brush his teeth, wash his face, and comb his hair.

Putting on a clean T-shirt and a pair of blue jean shorts, he quickly tied his tennis shoes. When he reached the kitchen, his mother greeted him.

"Good morning," she said, placing a bowl of cereal in front of him.

Climbing onto the stool at the bar, he replied, "Good morning, Mama. Thanks." After eating all his cereal, Elzafan drank the milk from the bowl. That was always the sweetest part!

Finishing up, he put the bowl and spoon in the kitchen sink before going outside to check on King. Making sure King had fresh food and water, he petted his best friend on the head and said, "I'll see you later, boy."

The big German Shepherd didn't even look up as he chowed down the food.

Elzafan went back inside and headed to his room for his school supplies. Grabbing his books off the dresser, he put them into the pack and strapped it to his back. He didn't notice that Johnny was hanging on to one of the books as he placed them into the bag. His mother gave him a quick hug and kiss on the cheek.

"Now, play nice. Your mama loves you," she said as she made sure his hair wasn't sticking up anywhere.

Now every time she told him to play nice, it meant for him to behave and be a good boy. "Okay, Mama. Love you too," he answered before going out the front door. The bus stop was right up the road, only about a four-minute walk.

Getting closer, he could see Jezia standing there waiting for him. She was smiling brightly as she waved at him. He smiled, waved back, and walked up to her.

"What's up, El? I didn't see you yesterday. Where were you?" She was always straight to the point.

"I was down at Big Pond," he replied.

Her brown eyes widened as she asked, "Did ya catch anything?"

Looking off in the distance, he answered, "A little." Before anything else could be said, the big orange bus pulled up. The air brakes hissed loudly as it finally came to a stop.

Now Jezia was very curious as she followed him onto the bus. She made sure to find a seat right beside him. "You actin' different, El. What's up with that?"

Knowing how persistent she could be, he would have to give her an answer. She'd never let it rest! "We'll talk about it later."

"All right then. How 'bout we meet at Votterbell's?"

"Okay. I'll meet you there this evening."

The bus came to another hiss-sounding halt, and the doors squeaked as they opened. Coming up the steps was another friend of Elzafan's. His name was Chow. Tall and slim, he had short black hair and wore small wire-framed glasses.

Seeing Elzafan, he walked down the aisle and sat in the seat behind him. Slightly leaning forward, he asked, "How are you, Elzafan?"

"I'm okay. How about you?"

Pressing his glasses on a little tighter with his index finger, he answered, "I was up late last night. Father and Mother needed help with Wang Lun." Chow's parents owned and operated this small Chinese restaurant. In English, *wang lun* means yellow moon. His father opened it before Chow was born and was able to buy the house that was right beside it. On very busy days, Chow would help with whatever needed to be done. Sometimes, he would clean up the dining area, wash dishes, or do some other needed tasks. This was one of the many ways Chow honored and appreciated his family. Being a straight-A student was another one!

Changing the subject, Chow replied, "Hey, if you want, maybe we could play some ping-pong this weekend."

"Yeah, that would be fun," Elzafan quickly answered. Now the first time he'd been to Chow's house, it was a great surprise. The large building behind his friend's house looked like a regular storage place. When Chow took him inside, however, it was totally different! There was a full-sized ping-pong table and a couple of video games. The place was like a small arcade! When Elzafan looked around at all the modern technology, he realized that Chow's family was rich. He remembered the day when Chow invited him into his home. In the living room, they had the biggest television that he had ever seen! He remembered thinking, *Maybe the restaurant next door helps them pay for all of these nice things.*

When the bus pulled up to the school, his thoughts were interrupted as they came to a stop. Everybody walked slowly in a single file line as they got off the bus.

"I'll see you after school," Elzafan said to Chow before heading to class. Since Jezia and he were in the same class, they walked together. Along the way, they would glance at each other and smile.

Jezia giggled each time they looked at each other. When they made it to class, everyone quickly found their seats.

Suddenly, the morning bell rang loudly. Elzafan could see Jezia looking at him with a big grin on her face. He knew she would have questions about why she didn't see him the day before. It wasn't like him to avoid her. In fact, he always loved being around her. He wanted to tell her everything with all his heart, but he didn't know how she would take it. What would she say if he told her about Zoayland? Would she think that he had lost his mind? These questions in his mind were interrupted when the teacher came in.

"Good morning, everyone," she said before taking a seat behind her desk.

"Good morning, Ms. Lawson," they all answered together.

After arranging some papers, she stood up and walked over to the large green chalkboard. Every student could hear the familiar sound of her writing with a piece of chalk. *Swoosh, tap, swoosh, tap*. When she stepped to the side of the board, everyone could see what was written. In big white letters, it read, My Happy Time.

"Your assignment is to write a short story or poem about a happy time you have had."

After the teacher said this, shuffling sounds could be heard as every girl and boy got out their writing materials.

Elzafan took out his composition book and lead pencil from his backpack and prepared to write. As he thought about some happy times he'd enjoyed, Johnny slowly crawled out of his pack and up the side of the desk. When the little red ant reached the desktop, Elzafan didn't notice him at first. He was about to write when he saw Johnny standing there on the paper right in front of him! Elzafan quickly looked around and leaned over, whispering, "How did you get here, Johnny?"

"Before you left Zoayland, I climbed into your bag."

"I'm so glad you came with me, Johnny, but why would you leave home?"

"You are my friend, Elzafan, and I thought you might need a friend too."

"Thanks, buddy. I want to talk more, but I have some work to do right now."

"I understand. We will talk later," Johnny replied before crawling back down the desk and into Elzafan's backpack.

Elzafan was still amazed that Johnny had returned with him, but he was very happy that he did! Refocusing on his assignment, Elzafan began his poem.

> For my happy time
> Big Pond is the place
> Of quiet and nice solitude
>
> With a small stream
> And pool of water
> Each visit just always seems new
>
> It's filled with fish
> From a pond above
> When it rains
> The water flows down
>
> Ofttime with my pal
> A shepherd named King
> Big Pond is the best place around
>
> For my happy time
> Big Pond is the place
> Where I can be free of all care
>
> Surrounded by woods
> Away from it all
> I'm happiest when I am there

Chapter 28

After getting home from school, Elzafan gave Johnny some water and a little piece of an apple to eat. They talked for a few minutes and Elzafan let him know that he would be back in a little while. Letting his mother know that he was going down the street for a little bit, she reminded him to take out the trash and take care of King before leaving.

Finishing these small chores, Elzafan crossed the street and made his way around the neighbor's house toward the apple tree. Climbing up the white fence, he grabbed a hold of the limb above and pulled himself up. As he sat there with his feet dangling, he saw Jezia running across her yard toward him. *That girl's fast*, he thought as she got closer. He had raced her many times before, and they were tied often.

Jezia climbed up onto the tree limb and sat beside him. Giving him a friendly kiss on his cheek, she said, "What's up El?"

Slightly blushing, he answered, "Hey Jezia." Every time she gave him a peck on the cheek, he could feel his heart speed up! It also caused him to forget what he was going to say at times.

Going straight to the point, she questioned him, "So why didn't I see ya yesterday?"

"Oh, I was down at Big Pond for a while and got back late."

"Did ya catch anything? I know you didn't go catchin' crawdads without me," she said with a big smile.

"I caught a fish but…"

Before he could finish, she quickly asked, "A brim? A bass?"

"It was a tiger fish."

Now she was curious. "I don't know what it is El, but somethin's different about you. For real…what's going on?"

"Okay. I went to Big Pond yesterday and as I stood there, a strong wind blew against me. I lost my balance and fell into the water. Through my fall, I have found the way, the truth, and the life."

"Boy, you've told me some strange stuff before, but this don't make any sense at all. What do you mean about findin' the way?"

After a moment of silence, he replied, "I have found the way to eternal life."

"And what is eternal life, El?"

"It is a spiritual life that will last forever." Elzafan could tell that she was thinking about what he had said, so he continued, "One day, we are going to leave this world. Have you ever thought about where we go after we die?"

"Well, yeah. When my grandma passed away, I thought about it. She always told me that her home was in heaven. So when you fell into the water, what happened then?"

Not sure how to answer, he replied, "I saw a light and started swimming toward it. When I reached the surface, it was a completely different place. At first, I thought it was only a dream, but it was another realm, like another world."

Jezia stared at him for a minute and said, "Really El? Why are you pulling my leg?" Giggling, she climbed down and looked up to him before leaving. "You had me goin' for a second, boy! I'll catch ya later." Before he could say another word, she took off running toward her house.

* * * * *

Climbing down out of the apple tree, Elzafan thought, *Well...that went a little different than I expected.* He was kind of surprised at how she responded. She thought he was just kidding around! Now it wasn't like him to just give her some tall tale. Maybe she would think about it and take him more seriously later.

He certainly wouldn't get in a hurry to bring it up again. After all, how many people would believe in a realm or world beyond this physical one where they live? Elzafan had even heard a grown-up say, "If I can't see it or feel it, then it doesn't exist." As for himself, he believed that two realms existed—the physical one that could be seen, and the spiritual one that was unseen. Walking back home, he went into the gate that led to his backyard.

King quickly met him and licked his hand to say hello.

Rubbing his buddy's head, he replied, "Jezia thinks I'm joking, boy. I guess for now it will be our little secret." Even though doubts and fears would come to his mind sometimes, he still had love and peace deep down on the inside. As he refilled King's water bucket, he began to hear a song in his mind that said,

> I was lost—in my sin,
> Then Your love—took me in.
> Lord, I thank You for grace,
> Now I seek Your Holy face.

Grace... Now he remembered her. Grace, the singing gray squirrel. Not exactly sure what grace was, Elzafan decided to ask his mother.

When he went back inside, she was at the kitchen sink stirring a jug of freshly made tea. He pulled up a seat at the bar and asked, "Mama, what is grace?"

"I've read in the Bible that God saves us by His grace." Rinsing and drying her hands, she continued, "Pastor Samuel out at the church says that grace is God's undeserved favor. How about we go out there Sunday morning?"

"I'd like that, Mama."

Surprised and happy that he was interested, she fixed him a glass of tea with ice and said, "I have something to give you." Going into her bedroom and returning to where he was sitting, she handed him a little light blue book. It had a flap with a snap button that kept it closed. On the spine, he read the words HOLY BIBLE.

Unsnapping and opening it, he asked, "Where did you get this, Mama?"

"It was your grandpa's Bible."

"Thank you, Mama. This is a treasure to me!" His mother had told him about the times his grandfather preached. His grandpa had passed away when he was about two years old, but he always loved hearing these stories about him. Closing and fastening the Bible shut, Elzafan finished drinking his tea and put the glass in the sink. "Thanks again, Mama."

She smiled. "You're welcome, Elzy Poo."

Picking up the Bible, he went down the hallway to his bedroom and quietly closed the door.

Chapter 29

"Oscar! Oscar!" Noofie screamed. "I just stopped by Johnny's. The Golden Leaf Scroll has been stolen!"

With a troubled look on his face, the little tiger fish replied, "Not good! Not good! The scroll is so dear. Johnny should know! This he must hear!"

Printed in the USA
CPSIA information can be obtained
at www.ICGtesting.com
CBHW041216230924
14725CB00056B/912

9 798887 511092